FOLLOW
YOUR HEART ♥

DISNEY

GIRL meets WORLD

FOLLOW YOUR HEART

Adapted by Alexa Young
Based on the series created by Michael Jacobs and April Kelly
Part One is based on the episode "Girl Meets Boy," written by Michael Jacobs
Part Two is based on the episode "Girl Meets Sneak Attack," written by Cindy Fang

DISNEY PRESS
Los Angeles · New York

Printed in the United States of America
First Edition, July 2015
1 3 5 7 9 10 8 6 4 2
Library of Congress Control Number: 2014956441
ISBN 978-1-4847-2812-3
G658-7729-4-15142

For more Disney Press fun, visit www.disneybooks.com
Visit DisneyChannel.com

SUSTAINABLE
FORESTRY
INITIATIVE

Certified Chain of Custody
Promoting Sustainable Forestry

www.sfiprogram.org
SFI-01054

The SFI label applies to the text stock

PART ONE

CHAPTER 1

Kids rushed through the halls of John Quincy Adams Middle School, paying no attention to each other as they played games and sent text messages on their cell phones. Riley Matthews and her best friend in the seventh grade (and the entire world), Maya Hart, stood by their lockers as the warning bell rang, signaling that there was only a few more minutes before class would begin. But Riley didn't care about making it to history. She was too busy thinking about her future—or at least the future she was hoping to have—with Lucas Friar.

Just then, as if Riley's brain had magically made

him appear, Lucas walked by. How was it possible that he looked even more adorable .that day than he had the day before? His dark blond hair was the perfect amount of messy, and his navy-blue sweater hugged his slightly muscular arms.

Lucas smiled as he passed, and Riley felt her heart beating so hard she wondered if her best friend could hear it. Lucas seemed so sweet and cool, all at the same time, as he continued on his way, swinging his army-green messenger bag onto his lap and sitting down on the bench in the middle of the indoor quad.

Riley felt positively giddy. She had to do something to make sure Lucas knew she was happy to see him. After all, he had just moved to New York City from Austin, Texas, and Riley's dad had always told her to make new kids feel welcome. So she punched a text message to Lucas into her brand-new smartphone, complete with shiny red case.

Maya looked at Riley and sighed. "Talk to him!" Maya insisted.

"Why?" Riley asked, reluctantly turning her attention away from her phone. She tilted her head and widened her eyes at Maya while hugging her books to her chest. "We have a great text relationship!"

"You know what's better than a text relationship?" Maya asked, placing her hands on her hips and shaking her long, wavy blond hair in frustration.

"What?" Riley asked.

"*Talk* to him!" Maya insisted with a serious, intense glare. Maya was always trying to get Riley to step outside of her comfort zone. But Riley wasn't interested in that. She was feeling too . . . comfortable.

Ding! A text message alert came chiming through Riley's phone. It was a reply! From Lucas! She smiled broadly as Maya rolled her eyes, beyond annoyed.

Riley held up her phone, hoping to silence Maya with what was clearly the most amazing text message exchange in the history of text message exchanges.

> **RILEY:** WHERE YOU GOIN?

> **LUCAS:** HISTORY. I SIT NEXT TO YOU.

Swoon. Things could not be going better between them. This was going to be the relationship to end all relationships! Riley turned away from Maya and sent another message.

> **RILEY:** SO DO I!! :) :)

Maya didn't seem impressed. "He's right over there!" she said to Riley.

"Nooo!" Riley shook her head at Maya. "Too complicated over there. Lots can go wrong over there. The only thing that can go wrong over here is if we go over there."

Maya wasn't having it. She held up an arm and pointed forcefully in the direction of Lucas, who was literally four feet away.

Riley sighed. Maybe Maya was right. Maybe she *should* go talk to Lucas. What could possibly go wrong . . . um, right? Riley handed her books to

Maya, with her phone sitting like a cherry on top of them, and slowly walked over to the bench where Lucas was seated, leaning against a low tiled wall. But she didn't sit next to him. *Obviously.* Instead, she crouched behind the wall and slowly peeked up from behind it, resting her chin on the smooth wood surface, just beside Lucas's shoulder.

Lucas was typing a reply to Riley's latest message, but now she couldn't write back to him, because she didn't have her phone. Oh, why had she listened to Maya? This was such a bad idea. Bad, bad, bad! Okay, fine. Maybe she should talk to him. Yes. She should talk to him. Definitely.

Hi. Riley mouthed the word, but no sound came out.

Hi! Riley attempted to speak again, but still nothing.

Hellooo . . . she tried, to no avail. It was as if she were the Little Mermaid, and the evil sea witch Ursula had stolen her voice, making it impossible for her to communicate with her one true love!

Riley cringed, chin still resting on the little

wall behind Lucas, and looked over at Maya. What bright new ideas would her best friend have for her now?

Maya cringed right back and then dramatically mouthed the words "Talk to him!" As if Riley hadn't heard Maya's advice a million times already.

All right, then. She would try again.

Hi! This time Riley fanned out her fingers like Maya had as she mouthed the word, hoping there might be some volume control in her hand. But no such luck.

Riley turned to look at Maya, who got a disgusted look on her face. Riley frowned, as disappointed in herself as Maya seemed to be. She had to do something to show her best friend she'd made an effort. She couldn't just leave Lucas like that. Not without smelling him first! She moved her face dangerously close to the back of his head and took a big, long whiff. Then she took another whiff. That sealed the deal. He was officially perfect. Not only did he look delicious, but he smelled just as good. Like freshly laundered clothes and blueberry muffins!

Riley looked over at Maya again, super pleased with herself for getting so close to Lucas. Maya smiled a tight smile and motioned for Riley to join her back at the lockers. Riley happily complied, rushing back over with a gleam in her brown eyes.

"How'd I do?" she asked with a proud toss of her long, dark hair.

"You smelled him," Maya said as she shoved Riley's books and smartphone back into her arms.

"Yup!" Riley nodded.

"You smelled him! That's what you did!"

Riley hugged her books to her chest. "I walk through life the way I walk through life," she said dreamily.

"Can we please talk about this?" Maya demanded.

But instead of responding, Riley simply grabbed her phone from the top of her pile of books and punched in a message as she walked away.

A chime sounded in the back pocket of Maya's

cutoff jean shorts, which she wore over black tights with lace-up boots. She pulled out her ancient flip phone only to discover a text message from Riley in old-fashioned block letters.

"'Nope'!" Maya rolled her pale blue eyes in disbelief as she read the message out loud. She shook her head and sighed as she followed Riley to class.

CHAPTER 2

Cory Matthews, also known as Riley's dad, also known as Riley's history teacher, stood at the front of the classroom. He wore a black blazer over a blue plaid shirt, and his normally friendly face wasn't looking so friendly as he waved a smartphone at the students with one hand and wagged his finger at them with the other.

"You guys don't connect with each other," Mr. Matthews said with a stern look in his dark eyes. "It's like you can't exist without these!"

The students blinked innocently back at him, their faces as blank as the screen on their teacher's powered-down phone.

"You use emoticons rather than emotions," he continued. "You're an unfeeling generation of zombies!"

Riley and Maya couldn't resist. They leaned toward each other while still seated at their desks and made loud, gurgling noises typical of the undead. Riley even pretended to go for a mouthful of Maya's brains as they both flailed around and rolled their eyes back into their heads.

"Stop eating her!" Mr. Matthews said, briefly joining in on the joke.

Riley and Maya giggled as the door at the front of the classroom opened.

"You're late, Miss Myzell!" Mr. Matthews said, turning around to reprimand the girl with the thick-rimmed glasses.

"My goldfish died," Myzell said flatly, casually tilting her head to one side and straightening the hot-pink jacket she wore over a matching pink top.

"You see, this is what I'm talking about!" Mr. Matthews told his students, wrapping an arm around the girl and shuttling her into the classroom. "Miss

Myzell has clearly suffered a tragic loss, yet she does not seem in touch with her actual emotions."

"Excuse me?" Myzell acted like she was offended. "I am crying my eyes out. I'm going to have to leave class early!" Mr. Matthews looked at her tear-free face, confused. With that, she spun on her heel and walked straight back out the door.

Wide-eyed, Mr. Matthews turned to his students. "Wow! She actually made it out the door this time!" He opened the door to go after Myzell, but she was already walking back inside.

"I actually made it out the door this time!" Myzell said, laughing, as she reentered the classroom and took her seat.

"Dad, adjust and deal," Riley said, getting back to the conversation they'd been having before their classmate's tardy arrival. "Cell phones have been around for, like, ever."

"It will amaze you to know that there was a whole world before you . . . and cell phones," Mr. Matthews replied.

"And it will amaze *you* to know that I have three

hundred ninety-four friends in here!" Riley said, holding up her smartphone and tapping a purple-painted fingernail against the screen.

"And I'm amazed that you *believe* that!" Mr. Matthews fired back.

Riley sighed and set the phone down on her desk as her dad drew a horizontal line straight across the green chalkboard.

"This is a timeline of all human existence," Mr. Matthews told the class before pointing to the left side of the line. "Starting here is everyone who ever lived, laughed, loved, and understood the value of life. The cell phone era, which begins right around here," he continued, striking a heavy vertical mark near the end of the timeline, "pretty much destroys all that. Way to go, *you*!"

"Sir?" Lucas raised his hand with a politeness that matched his southern accent. "If I may take a different position?"

"Yeah, save me, Mr. Friar. Do I go too far?" Mr. Matthews asked.

"Always, sir." Lucas nodded, and Riley gave him

a supportive smile. "I understand your point, but I use my phone to video-chat with my old friends and to find out what's going on in Texas."

"Yeah," Maya chimed in with a smirk before putting on her thickest Texas drawl. "How else can he keep tabs on all the hoedowns and cattle pageants?"

"Maya—" Riley scolded her friend for being so harsh.

"It's okay, Riley," Lucas insisted. "I'm unaffected by Maya's views of country life. As my uncle Buster always says, 'be like an eagle and soar above the mockingbird.'"

"You're the mockingbird!" Riley whispered to Maya with a big grin.

"I know," Maya muttered under her breath before turning around in her chair to glare at Lucas, raising her hands and curling her fingers to demonstrate how desperately she wanted to strangle him. "It kills me that I can't get to you!"

"Sorry, ma'am," Lucas replied with a sweet, unaffected smile, lifting a hand to his forehead and tipping an imaginary cowboy hat in Maya's direction.

"Oooh!" Maya fumed, beyond annoyed.

Riley, on the other hand, felt all tingly and warm inside every time she looked at Lucas. She was so glad he wasn't in Texas anymore!

"Farkle time, sir?" interjected Farkle, Riley's freckle-faced friend, raising his hand to get Mr. Matthews's attention.

"Oh, I love Farkle time!" Mr. Matthews replied, giddily clasping his hands together and heading for the boy's desk.

Farkle marched up to the front of the classroom. His straight reddish-brown hair was brushed forward so it hung like a helmet atop his head.

"With all due respect to history, Mr. Matthews, what's important to our generation will be on *this* side of the timeline." Farkle turned and pointed to the far right of the chalkboard before adding: "When Farkle and technology *rule*!"

Continuing with his lecture, Farkle walked over to Riley, seated at her desk in the front row. "And I will easily be able to make another one of *you*," he noted, plucking a hair from Riley's head. She yelped out in pain. "And another one of *you*!" he said, turning to Maya and plucking out one of her hairs, eliciting the same pained response. Farkle nodded, satisfied.

"Wait, so now there's four of us and one of you?" Riley asked Farkle, tilting her head in Maya's direction.

"That's awesome!" Farkle beamed like a mad scientist as Riley and Maya scrunched up their faces at each other. "The future! You can't escape it! I am Farkle!" he shouted, raising his arms in a triumphant victory pose—a classic Farkle move. Then he marched back to his desk and took his seat as Mr. Matthews vacated it and returned to the front of the classroom.

"The assignment! *You* can't escape it! I am teacher!" Mr. Matthews smiled before shifting back into serious mode. "Okay, so here's what we're going to do, guys. We are going to split into teams and discover whether or not new technology has made us better people. You'll do presentations on your findings, and here's a twist: no computers."

"*What?*" Farkle screamed, slamming his hands down on his desk and glaring at the teacher.

"We're going old-school," Mr. Matthews explained. "You're going to do your research at the New York Public Library."

"Where?" Maya demanded, but Mr. Matthews just kept talking.

"And here's another twist, because I trust you . . . not at all," he said, reaching out his hands. "Give me your cell phones."

"No!" Riley shouted.

The class erupted in a chorus of complaints. They didn't want their cell phones taken away. It wasn't fair! How could he do this to them?

But Mr. Matthews insisted. He walked from one row of desks to the next as the students reluctantly handed over their beloved electronic devices.

"Thank you," Mr. Matthews said. "Okay, so, our teams for this assignment will be Maya—"

The moment her name was called, Farkle leapt

into Maya's lap. "What up?" he asked flirtatiously. Maya pushed him off and shoved him back toward his seat. But the deal was done. They were team number one.

"And, Riley, you will be with—" Mr. Matthews glanced around the room as Lucas raised his eyebrows and waved sweetly at Riley, silently volunteering to be her partner.

"No!" Mr. Matthews said. He didn't want his daughter teaming up with the boy she was obviously crushing on. Before he even had a chance to break them up, however, the rest of the students formed teams on their own and then the bell rang. Too late. Class dismissed!

"No!" Mr. Matthews said, louder this time, as the students all gathered up their things and headed for the door. When Lucas walked by, Mr. Matthews glared at him and fumed, "Why did you have to come here?"

"Sorry I make you uneasy, sir," Lucas replied with a gentle smile.

"Oh, Dad, we don't even have our phones." Riley

grinned reassuringly at her father as Lucas left the classroom. "I mean, what could possibly happen?"

Of course she was already imagining all the amazing things that could happen now that she and Lucas would be working on their first official assignment together. But she didn't want to make her dad feel worse than he already seemed to feel.

CHAPTER 3

As students slammed their lockers closed and shuffled off to their classes, Riley and Maya stood in the middle of the quad, talking about the crazy assignment Riley's dad had just given them—and how cool it was that Riley and Lucas were going to be partners.

"Hey, soaring eagle," Maya called out when she noticed Lucas making his way through the crowded hall. "You walking with us to the library tonight?"

"Sure, if that's good with you guys?" Lucas asked. He stopped and stood next to a bank of yellow lockers.

"Well, seeing as how you're *Riley's* partner on this assignment," Maya said with a glint in her big blue eyes, "I guess we should find out if it's okay with her." Maya turned and smiled at Riley like a cat who'd just eaten a very tasty canary.

Riley stood there, trying not to panic. Lucas grinned at her. He was clearly waiting for her to say something, but she was right back in mute Little Mermaid mode. She couldn't move, let alone speak. Her heart was beating faster than ever, drowning out any possible hint of a thought in her head as she looked at Lucas, with his golden skin, his sparkling green eyes. He was so tall, so cute, so perfectly . . . perfect.

"Riley . . . ?" Maya asked.

Riley swallowed down the lump in her throat but still couldn't come up with anything to say.

"Riley," Maya said again. "Any thoughts on this . . . that might come out of your mouth . . . in *word form?*"

Riley puffed out her lips with an exaggerated, helpless frown as Maya continued: "No, because you don't have your phone anymore, so what are you going to do to communicate, I wonder?"

Finally, Riley managed to raise her thumbs in the air. That was a good start, right?

"Well, look at that. Two thumbs up from Riley," Maya said as Riley's face slowly broke into a big grin. "And a smiley face!"

Lucas smiled back at Riley and headed off to class.

There. Done! Plans to study at the library were officially made—and Riley hadn't even needed to use spoken words *or* texted ones. Take that, Dad!

CHAPTER 4

The Matthews family sat around the dinner table in their apartment, sharing the details of the day between bites of roast chicken and mashed potatoes.

"It was a good day," said Riley's little brother, Auggie.

Mr. Matthews smiled and nodded at his adorable son, encouraging him to go on.

"And then my friends treated me nicely. And then my teacher measured us. And then I'm growing. And then. Jenny Lewis. *Loves* me!" Auggie made a grand, sweeping gesture with his hand when he revealed this juicy detail. His brown chin-length curls bounced as he thought for a moment about Jenny's affection, and then he quickly declared: "I think because I'm growing."

Everyone grinned at the little guy, who could always be counted on to entertain them. But then Riley remembered that she was still upset with her dad.

"It *wasn't* a good day," Riley insisted, launching into an Auggie-style report of her own. "And then my friend pulled my hair out. And then my teacher took my phone away. And then my teacher was also my father!" She pointed an accusatory finger at her dad, who furrowed his brow.

"At least you're growing," Auggie pointed out in a completely unhelpful manner.

"Honey, please don't come apart," said Riley's mom, Topanga Matthews. "Look at this as a beautiful opportunity to spend time with your family!"

Riley sighed and glanced over at Auggie. Her parents both nodded awkwardly and looked at Auggie, too. Yeah. Great. What kind of beautiful opportunity was this?

"Hello, Riley," Auggie offered sweetly.

"How ya doing?" Riley fought the urge to roll her eyes.

"Wanna hear about my day?" Auggie asked. "It was a good day—"

"Mom!" Riley glared at her mother.

"Forgive her, Auggie," said Mrs. Matthews. "She misses her telephone."

"Well, then she can have mine!" Auggie held up a big purple toy with a neon-green antenna and handed it across the table.

Riley pressed a button on the device, causing it to beep and crackle before a mechanical voice came through the speaker, saying, "The cow goes . . ."

"Mooo!" Auggie replied, right on cue.

"I'm not gonna make it," Riley groaned through gritted teeth, exasperation flashing in her dark eyes.

"That's what your father thinks," Mrs. Matthews said.

"She can't," Mr. Matthews agreed, taking a bite of chicken.

"Honey, please don't make your father right,"

Mrs. Matthews begged. "It's no good for any of us when your father is right."

"She's right," Mr. Matthews said.

Riley tried to stare down her dad, but he just smiled back at her.

"Why are you *really* doing this?" Riley demanded.

"Because I want you and your friends to become human beings," Mr. Matthews insisted. "And I believe that by doing this, you guys can learn to become real human beings."

Before Riley could get even angrier with her father, a loud buzz echoed through the apartment, and a voice came through the intercom: "Hey, losers, it's Maya!"

"Except her," Mr. Matthews said, pointing toward the intercom.

"You know what?" Riley got up from the table and walked across the room to the intercom. "I *am* going to do this. I can get through this whole thing without making a text or a call!" She pressed the buzzer and told Maya to come on up.

"Of course you can, sweetheart." Mrs. Matthews got up from the table, walked over to Riley, and put an arm around her. "And you know what? You're already a wonderful human being, but every so often little tests like this are going to come up."

"Why?" Riley frowned.

"Because it's your father's job to give you little tests," Mrs. Matthews replied. "And maybe, along the way, you guys are going to learn a little bit more about yourselves."

Just then, Maya came bursting through the door. "Yeah, like I've learned that I'm actually really okay with all of this."

"You don't miss your phone, Maya?" Mrs. Matthews asked.

"I was the only one in class without a smartphone anyway," Maya said, still holding on to the brass doorknob as she shrugged. "Now I kind of feel like everybody's even."

The intercom buzzer sounded again, followed by a slightly nasal voice: "Farkle!"

"Be ready in a minute," Riley replied tersely.

Yet another buzz came through the intercom, followed by a much cuter voice: "And Lucas . . ."

"Ready now!" Riley squealed, tearing through the apartment. She grabbed her favorite army-green jacket with the black hood from the hook by the door and raced out, dragging Maya with her.

"Didja see that?" Mr. Matthews demanded when the girls were gone, shaking his fork at his wife across the dinner table and launching into a rapid-fire tirade: "Y'know what that was? That was boys! Too soon for boys. Not ready for boys. I don't want boys. We just gonna accept boys?"

"It happened. She's gone. She was nice. We had fun. But we still have *him*," Mrs. Matthews cooed, reaching over to grab Auggie by the arm excitedly. "You wanna color?"

"Color!" Auggie practically sang, clapping his hands together.

"Of course you do!" Mrs. Matthews cheered, grabbing art supplies from a metal cart next to the kitchen counter while Mr. Matthews started clearing dishes from the table. "Let's color for the rest of our lives!"

As Mrs. Matthews took out a yellow crayon and began to draw on a piece of construction paper, Auggie looked up and batted his long, dark lashes. "Will I be getting a real cell phone someday?"

"Someday," Mrs. Matthews replied.

"Dominic Falconi has a real cell phone," Auggie said, widening his brown eyes at his mom.

"Would you rather have a real cell phone or would you rather color with us?" Mrs. Matthews asked. Mr. Matthews looked on and nodded at his son, confident Auggie would give them the answer they were hoping for.

"Color with you," Auggie dutifully replied with a smile.

Yes! Mr. and Mrs. Matthews pumped their arms victoriously.

"Does *that* get me a cell phone?" Auggie added, and his parents' faces fell with disappointment.

"Not too much longer with this one, either," Mrs. Matthews said glumly to her husband.

"Well, you'll always have me," he replied.

"Yeah." Mrs. Matthews forced a smile, took a deep breath, and got back to coloring with Auggie, hoping against hope that she could draw something so magical that he would never want to leave.

Or at least not ask for a cell phone again for a very, very long time.

CHAPTER 5

Walking through the dark, dingy halls of the New York Public Library's Greenwich Village branch, Riley and her friends couldn't help feeling like they had somehow fallen through a portal that had swept them back in time. Farkle was first, with Riley, Maya, and Lucas following close behind in a single-file line.

"What *is* this place?" Riley practically gasped when she saw the immense shelves of books towering over them, stretching all the way up to the improbably high ceiling.

"This is where the ancients stored all of their wisdom," Farkle replied in a hushed tone, nodding in wide-eyed wonder as he took it all in.

"Look at all those . . ." Maya paused, searching for the right word.

"Books!" Farkle offered.

"Boo-ooks," Maya and Riley said, marveling, like cavemen discovering fire.

"Look," Lucas said. He grabbed a thick volume from a shelf and blew on the cover, releasing a thick cloud of dust that allowed him to read the title. *"Tales of Human Interaction."*

"We'll take it!" Maya plucked the book away from Lucas and dropped it onto a nearby table. "Thanks, Quick Draw!"

Maya sat down with Farkle and slid the book along the dark wood surface toward him. "Farkle, do whatever ya do with that."

"You mean read?" Farkle flipped open the book while Riley and Lucas remained standing and looked on from behind. "Chapter one—"

"Oh, I'm bored out of my *mind*! Let's go to a movie," Maya suggested before Farkle could read any further.

"Shhh!" A sudden harsh, hissing noise nearly caused all four of them to jump out of their skin.

They gasped, completely startled to see an elderly woman standing behind a tall desk on the other side of the room. She was dressed in black, her pale hair pulled back in a tight bun. It was so deathly quiet in the creepy old building, they hadn't realized anybody else was around.

"There's one of those ancients now," Farkle whispered. He leapt up and raced over to talk to the woman, with the others following. "Oh, wondrous gatekeeper of the knowledge, we are travelers from another time and place," Farkle told her.

"Seventh-grade middle school," Riley added, waving her arms at the woman like a servant might fan an Egyptian princess.

The woman offered no reply but simply peered at the group through a pair of dark-rimmed glasses perched at the end of her nose.

"We wish to partake of this information from your great hall of wisdom," Farkle tried to explain.

"Do you rent phones?" Riley quickly interjected.

"Shhh!" the woman hissed more harshly this time, pressing a finger to her lips and leaning over her desk threateningly.

"There's no one here but us," Lucas said, confused.

"Yeah, why do we have to shush?" Maya demanded.

"I'll handle this, Maya," Farkle insisted. He held up a hand to quiet his friends, who had gathered in a cluster behind him. Then he turned back to the woman and tilted his head coyly, going into smooth-and-flirty Farkle mode. "She obviously likes it quiet." He gazed deeply into the woman's eyes and continued, "Hellooo, book lady."

"Well, hello," the woman said in a pinched voice. "And who might you be?"

"I might be Farkle."

"Would you do me a favor, Farkle?"

"Oh, you know I will." Farkle leaned in close, laying on the charm.

"Why don't you go over *there*," the woman said,

pointing to a table before raising the same finger to her lips to add, "and *shhh!*"

"Well, that's disappointing." Farkle sniffed, defeated.

Maya grabbed Farkle by the arm and dragged him back over to the table, where they began to search through their book for something to put in their report. Riley and Lucas trailed behind, unsure what to do—or say—next.

"So . . ." Riley offered as she stood next to Lucas, nervously kicking the toe of one of her black ankle boots into the carpet.

"Yeah . . ." Lucas glanced at Riley and quickly turned away.

"Uh-huh," Riley offered, fixing her gaze on the ground.

"This chapter is called 'Disconnect to Connect,'" Farkle read aloud to Maya.

"'Not until we put down our phones, switch off our computers, and look in each other's eyes will we be able to touch each other's hearts,'" Maya read, and then added with a smirk, "Yeah, like that's going to work on anybody!"

As Riley turned toward Lucas, he turned to her, and just like that, they looked into each other's eyes. They still weren't saying anything, but for that one brief, amazing moment, it was as if they were the only two people in the entire world. Riley had never felt so connected to anyone before.

No way. Was *this* what her dad had been talking about? Was *this* what Farkle and Maya's book was talking about? Suddenly, the whole crazy assignment was seeming a lot less crazy.

CHAPTER 6

Moonlight streamed down, illuminating Farkle's and Maya's faces as they sat in a massive bay window at the library. Maya leaned against the wall with a yellow legal pad perched on her thigh. She gazed through the giant pane of glass and sketched the night sky while Farkle stared at the bookshelves.

"People used to need places like this," Farkle told Maya. "But now we can hold everything that's here in a little device we can put in our pockets. I don't even need to look out this window to know what phase the moon is in or where the stars are."

"Yeah, well, I don't have a phone like that," Maya

replied while continuing to look out the window and draw. "I just have the actual sky."

"Oh. I'm so sorry for you—you're at a real disadvantage," Farkle said glumly before brightening a bit. "That can be the basis of our presentation! Okay? Want to read back the notes?"

"What notes?" Maya asked, still working on her sketch.

"You weren't taking notes?" Farkle demanded.

"No."

"Yeah, why bother?" Farkle said. "Without a computer, all we have is a pencil and a pad. What could we possibly do with *that*?"

Farkle grabbed the pad of paper from Maya and a look of awe washed over his face as he saw what she'd been working on. She had perfectly captured the full moon and night sky full of stars, the silhouettes of the towering buildings and lush treetops. It was beautiful. More beautiful than anything Farkle had seen on a computer or smartphone.

"Maya?" Farkle finally said, amazed at what his

friend had been able to do with the pencil and paper he had thought were so useless. "I had no idea."

"Yeah," Maya replied with a shrug and a smile. "Neither did I."

♥ ♥ ♥

Sitting at the long library table, Riley and Lucas pored over books about the history of human communication. It was crazy to think that there was a time not that long before when people didn't have *any* kind of phones. If they wanted to tell somebody something, they had to actually go over to that person's house—or write a letter!

"My dad thinks that we have no idea how to talk to each other," Riley said, looking over at Lucas.

"What if he's right?" Lucas asked quietly.

"*Shhh!*" hissed the old lady from behind the library desk.

"But we're not saying anything," Lucas said to the woman, shocked that she could even hear them from that far away.

"I know!" the woman fired back.

"Then why are you shushing us?" Riley asked.

"Because I can't take it anymore! You guys are hopeless! Come here!" The woman motioned to Riley, who marched over to see what she wanted. "A couple of sweet kids like you, and you sit there like a couple of lumps. You're a disgrace to every single story on these shelves!"

"Okay, so what do I say to him?" Riley asked.

"Look around!" the woman said. "There's nothing here but books about boys and girls and men and women and what they say to each other. Open any one of them and—"

Riley reached down to take a look at one of the books the woman had been reading.

"No!" the woman snapped, and pushed Riley's hand away. "Not that one."

Now Riley *really* wanted to see what she was reading. She reached out and tried to grab another book, but the woman was too quick.

"Ho boy! Not that one!" she said again, shoving

the books under her desk. "Look, all of these books have one thing in common."

"What's that?" Riley asked.

"They start on page one. Then each page you turn brings you deeper into the story. What's your name?"

"Riley."

"What's *his* name?"

"Lucas."

"You like a good story, Riley?" the woman asked, and Riley nodded. "Then start at the beginning," the woman said.

It sounded like such a no-brainer. Riley knew that she and Lucas could have a story—a potentially *amazing* story—ahead of them. But it was never going to be told unless she took that leap and talked to him. *Really* talked to him. So she took the first step. She walked over to him. And then, finally, she said it.

"Hi." Riley smiled down at Lucas.

"Hi." Lucas smiled back.

That was it. Their story was finally beginning!

Riley sat back down at the table and shivered with excitement. She couldn't wait to see what would happen next.

♥ ♥ ♥

"'Because it's not until you've really looked at each other, and made a human connection, that you can even begin to know each other,'" Maya read aloud to Farkle in the window seat.

"Look at my eyes," Farkle said.

"No," Maya replied, staring down at the book.

"Look at my *eyes*," Farkle repeated more eagerly.

"No!" Maya fired back.

"Look at my eyes!" Farkle insisted.

"No!"

Okay, fine, Farkle decided. He didn't need to follow that old book's advice, anyway.

♥ ♥ ♥

Once they started talking, Riley and Lucas couldn't stop. And Riley loved hearing all about the stuff Lucas had done back home in Austin.

"I guess the thing I miss most about Texas are the pets I used to have," Lucas said.

"I had a hamster," Riley revealed.

"I had twenty-four horses."

"You win." Riley smiled. "Tell me about them."

"One day, after school, Sofia was foaling."

"That means she was giving birth, right?"

"Not too bad, city girl." Lucas looked genuinely impressed, and Riley giggled at his response. "And there was no one there, so I called Dr. Galendo, and he talked me through it."

Lucas paused and they both sat there for a moment, just staring into each other's eyes, until a hint of awkwardness crept back in.

"Anyway, that was it," Lucas added quickly.

But Riley didn't want that to be it. "More," she insisted.

"Did you know that a baby horse stands in the first hour after it's born?" Lucas asked.

"Really? I'd like to have been there for that."

"The coolest thing I've ever seen, and *I* was a part of it."

Once again, there was a pause in the conversation, and this time, as they stared at each other, it felt more natural. It was getting less scary. Not as uncomfortable. In fact, it was almost starting to feel like they'd known each other their whole lives.

"Riley?" Lucas finally broke the silence.

"Lucas?" Riley replied, her brown eyes widening with dreamy anticipation.

"I've never told this to anybody before."

Oh. My. Gosh. This was going to be big. Really big.

"Yeah?" Riley couldn't wait for him to say what he was going to say.

"I think . . ." Lucas said slowly, "someday . . . I might like to be a veterinarian."

Oh.

"That's cool, too," Riley responded with a slightly embarrassed grin.

"I delivered this beautiful palomino," Lucas recalled. "I'd show you her picture but . . . I don't have my phone."

"That's okay. Just keep talking." Riley encouraged

him with her biggest smile yet, resting her head on her hand and giving him her undivided attention.

While Lucas and Riley got deeper and deeper into their conversation, Maya continued to read to Farkle in the window seat: "'There is no connection you can make with any screen that compares to the moment you understand only human beings have souls.'"

"I have a soul," Farkle said.

"No." Maya clearly suspected otherwise.

"I *do*."

"No," Maya said flatly.

"I *do*!"

Maya looked quizzically at Farkle, like she might be ready to believe him. But then she thought better of it. She absolutely couldn't bring herself to buy what he was selling.

"No," she concluded.

Some human connections simply didn't make sense. But while Maya and Farkle weren't computing, Riley and Lucas most definitely were.

CHAPTER 7

Back at the Matthews apartment, arts and crafts were helping make the family connections stronger than ever.

"I colored a new picture," Auggie announced, leaping into his dad's lap.

"Stay like this forever," Mrs. Matthews begged her son.

"Wouldja please?" Mr. Matthews agreed, hugging Auggie close. "That'd be great."

"The picture's over *there*," Auggie said, rattling a cupful of crayons and pointing across the apartment.

Mr. and Mrs. Matthews followed Auggie over to a redbrick and no-longer-bare white wall. There, just above the dark wood baseboards, Auggie had drawn three stick figures along with two blue clouds and a red sun. He pointed at his artwork and proudly described what he'd drawn: "Mommy, Daddy, Auggie, and *no* Riley!"

"Uh, Auggie, I don't know if you should—" Mr. Matthews began, but before he could continue, Mrs. Matthews interrupted.

"It's beautiful!" she declared, silencing her husband. She didn't want to get angry about a few scribbles on the wall and squash their little boy's blossoming creativity. She turned to Mr. Matthews and quickly explained, "I think that's what you're supposed to do. I have no idea."

"And look at the 'frigerator!" Auggie said, pointing toward the kitchen.

"The *new* one?" Mrs. Matthews gasped.

They all turned to look at the large stainless-steel appliance, which was now completely covered in brightly colored swirls and scribbles. "That's our trip to the Jersey Shore!" Auggie explained.

"It's beautiful, it's . . . *beautiful*," Mrs. Matthews

forced herself to say through gritted teeth as she went to take a closer look and then shuttled Auggie off to his room. "I think that's what you're supposed to do."

As Mr. Matthews drew in a deep breath and shook his head at the new apartment décor, Riley walked in. She closed the front door behind her and leaned against it with a dreamy, far-off look in her eyes.

Mr. Matthews squinted at his daughter, completely confused. But Mrs. Matthews, who was now spraying the refrigerator and scrubbing it with a paper towel, smiled knowingly.

"How was your night, Riley?" Mr. Matthews asked, still looking baffled.

"Thank you for sending us to the library," Riley replied.

"Really?"

"Yes!" Riley walked over to Mr. Matthews. "Lucas and I did really well on the assignment. I *think* that we connected."

"What do you mean, 'connected'? What are

you talking about? How did you connect?" Mr. Matthews crossed his arms and tried not to cringe as he grilled Riley.

"We talked about stuff that was important to us," Riley explained. "Too important to text."

Mrs. Matthews, still scrubbing at the refrigerator, nodded proudly at her little girl—who wasn't so little anymore.

Riley continued to tell Mr. Matthews about her night. "Did you know that when you listen to someone, they'll tell you stuff?"

Mr. Matthews got a pained look on his face. "Oh, boy."

"Friends talk to each other, but real friends listen." Riley paused for a moment, thinking back on what an amazing night she'd had. "Maya knows how to draw. And I know how to be a real friend."

Mr. Matthews stood there, dumbfounded, his mouth wide open in shock.

"You're a good teacher, Dad. You can keep my phone as long as you want."

With that, Riley collapsed into her father's arms

and gave him a huge, grateful hug before heading off to her room to get ready for bed.

"Congratulations, Cory!" Mrs. Matthews said, walking over to where her husband stood in the middle of the living room.

"What did I do?" he demanded.

"You just taught our daughter how to feel."

"I did that?"

"You did." Mrs. Matthews widened her eyes and nodded happily.

"I didn't mean to do that."

"Well, you did."

"She has feelings now?" Mr. Matthews didn't want to believe it.

"Uh-huh."

"How many?"

"All of them."

"Well, put 'em back!"

"We can't do that."

Mr. Matthews thought for a moment. "I have a way."

"There's no way," Mrs. Matthews insisted.

"I have a way!" Mr. Matthews insisted, wagging his finger at his wife.

It might not have been the best way. It might not have even been a good way, but it was a way. As far as Mr. Matthews was concerned, it was the *only* way.

CHAPTER 8

The next morning in history class, Mr. Matthews urgently handed his students' cell phones back to them, one by one.

"Here you go, take your phone, take it now, very good," he insisted, forcing Riley's phone into her hand before moving along to Maya. "Here's your phone, good, great."

Once the phones were all back with their rightful owners, Mr. Matthews declared, "Nobody talks to nobody, no more feelings, thank you!" He took a deep, relieved breath and then moved on to the day's assignment. "Okay, guys, the great technology debate. Let's boot it up."

Maya and Farkle made an odd couple as they walked to the front of the classroom to begin their presentation. She was rocker chic in a black motorcycle jacket over a green-and-black-checkered shirt with silver spikes on it, while Farkle was in his usual neatly pressed khakis with an argyle sweater over a bright yellow turtleneck.

"I have always believed technology would help us fulfill our potential as a species," began Farkle, holding up his smartphone. "But when Farkle *does* rule the world, no matter what devices we come up with, we should also never forget what we can do with a pencil, a piece of paper, and our own imaginations."

Farkle reached into his pocket and pulled out a piece of paper, unfolding it carefully so he could show it to the class. "I've been keeping this in my pocket, where my phone used to be," he told them, holding up the sketch that Maya had done the previous night at the library. "I keep looking at it."

Farkle stared down at the picture for a few moments. It seemed like he might get choked up as

Maya, artist extraordinaire, stood there with thumbs tucked into the front pockets of her jeans.

Finally, Farkle said, "I'm fine."

"Thanks, Farkle." Maya glanced at her friend with a sheepish grin.

Unable to resist the moment, Farkle snapped back to attention. "Look at my eyes!" he said to Maya.

"No!" she replied, turning away, grateful that Riley and Lucas were standing there, about to begin their own presentation.

"I thought my whole life was in my phone," Riley began, fumbling with the device in her hands as she spoke. "But it turns out I don't have any friends in here—and you don't need your phone to connect with your real friends."

Mr. Matthews was beaming with pride as Lucas said, "Allow us to demonstrate."

Lucas and Riley turned to face each other.

"Hi," Riley said, looking directly into Lucas's eyes.

"Hi," Lucas replied.

That was it. That was all they needed to say. The message was so simple, yet it was one that needed to be communicated not via text but in person.

♥ ♥ ♥

Later that evening, Mr. Matthews went sneaking through the New York Public Library, looking for something—or someone. He walked up to a shelf of books, reaching up high to clear away a few so he could peer through to the other side.

"I'm not that tall," a female voice said.

So Mr. Matthews tried a lower shelf. A *much* lower shelf.

"Really?" the voice demanded.

Finally, just below his own eye level, he pushed aside some books to reveal . . . Maya!

"How ya doin'?" Maya said, smiling.

"You will keep an eye on Riley at all times," Mr. Matthews replied, cutting right to the chase. "You will send me message alerts. You will send me pictures."

Maya fought back a chuckle. "You're really scared, aren't you?"

"I'm a father," Mr. Matthews replied softly.

"Yeah. They're just friends," Maya said, trying to reassure him.

"Believe me, I know the story," Mr. Matthews told her. After all, he and Riley's mom had started out as friends, too. He just wasn't ready to let his little girl go. Not now. Not yet.

"But you're forgetting, I don't have the technology," Maya reminded Mr. Matthews. Sure, she had her old flip phone back, but that thing couldn't take and send pictures or anything like what he wanted.

"Now you do." Mr. Matthews placed a small black box on the bookshelf between them.

What was this? Maya walked around the bookcase to where Mr. Matthews stood, and reached out to take the box. She flipped open the top and discovered a shiny new smartphone inside. She took the phone out of the box and stared at it for a moment.

"You got me a phone?"

"My motives are completely selfish," Mr. Matthews admitted.

"I'm not sure they are, Mr. Matthews," Maya replied with a grimace. He'd always been like a dad to her, and now there he was, giving her a phone—just like a real dad would.

"Well, I also got you these." Mr. Matthews produced something else from behind his back. It was the coolest-looking art kit Maya had ever seen!

"Colored pencils?" She gazed at the gift, already thinking about all the amazing things she'd be able to do with it.

"Yeah." Mr. Matthews smiled. "You let me know everything that's going on with Riley, and if something beautiful ever happens? Paint me a picture."

Now *that* was something Maya could definitely do.

Did Auggie really think I could text Lucas on a toy phone?!?

The New York Public Library: where people went before smartphones existed.

Unfortunately, the book lady was immune to Farkle's charms.

Lucas and I had to disconnect to connect—and it made me very nervous!

Farkle thought Maya was taking notes for their presentation . . .

. . . but instead, she was drawing this amazing picture!

I learned that there really is something to be said for actual conversation. *Sigh*

And that sometimes your parents do know what they're talking about.

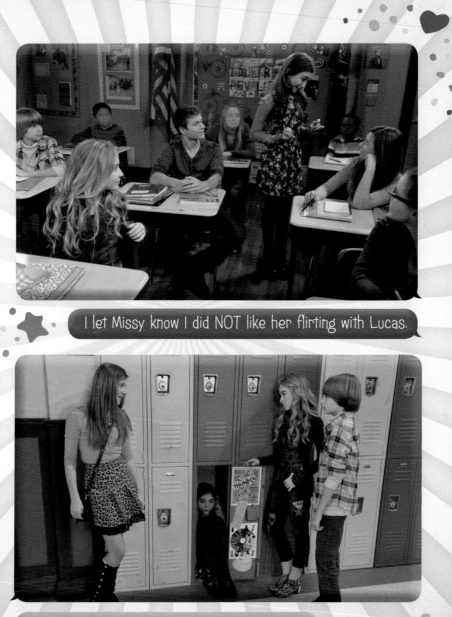

I let Missy know I did NOT like her flirting with Lucas.

Missy came over and said Lucas was into her.
I told my friends, "I live here now."

I felt like I couldn't face the world again. Ever.

We were like, *Do you think he'll sit with us or her?*

Farkle tried to steal Missy from Lucas with a signature flirting move.

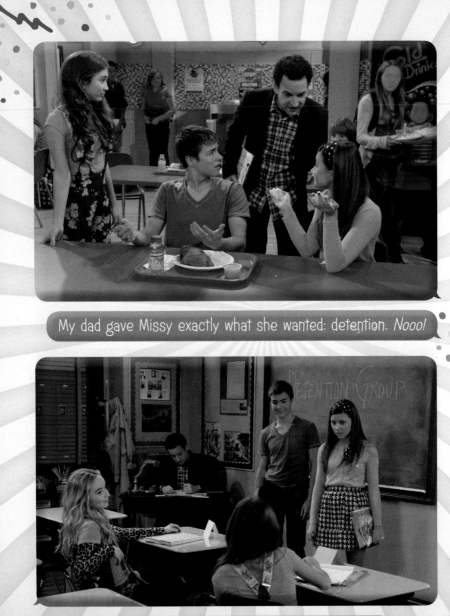

My dad gave Missy exactly what she wanted: detention. *Nooo!*

Missy was surprised to see me in the detention group.
Who's the sneaky one now?

PART
TWO

CHAPTER 1

Morning sunlight streamed into the cozy apartment as Mrs. Matthews stood over the dining table, spooning freshly made oatmeal from a blue pot into large yellow bowls.

"Hey, honey! What's for breakfast?" Mr. Matthews asked with a wave as he stood in the doorway leading into the kitchen. He wore a blue bathrobe over a gray T-shirt, and his face was covered in shaving cream.

Mrs. Matthews laughed at her husband and continued to spoon oatmeal into bowls as Auggie appeared behind his father.

"Hey, honey! What's for breakfast?" Auggie

echoed his dad. He, too, wore a blue bathrobe over a gray T-shirt, and his face was also covered in shaving cream.

"Awww, it looks like Auggie's trying to be Daddy's little man." Mrs. Matthews smiled as her husband and son walked up to the table.

"Yeah, so come over here and give Papa a smooch!" Auggie replied, marching over to Mrs. Matthews, who shook her head and laughed.

"Oh, yeah!" Mr. Matthews joked, approaching his wife from the other side. "Come over here and give Papa a smooch!"

As father and son got dangerously close to Mrs. Matthews, her blue eyes widened with panic and she backed away from them.

"No! I'm in the middle of a case, I have to be at the courthouse early, and I can't have shaving cream—"

But it was too late. When Mrs. Matthews lowered herself away from her husband, she got down just far enough that both Auggie and his dad were able to rub their faces against hers, covering her cheeks and hair with thick white foam.

"Ugh. All over my face!" Mrs. Matthews lamented.

"Nice job," Auggie said to his dad, holding out his hand.

"Pleasure doing business with ya," Mr. Matthews replied, giving his little boy's hand a shake.

They all grabbed kitchen towels and wiped off their faces as a buzzer sounded on the other side of the apartment and two voices came through the intercom.

"Maya," the first voice said.

"Farkle," came the second.

"Those are my friends," Riley said brightly, practically bouncing through the hall door. She had had the best night's sleep ever, and now she was ready for the best day ever.

"I love my friends!" Riley leapt down a step and into the living room. "It's a sunny day!" She smiled and breezed through the apartment toward the front door. "I love a sunny day." She hit the intercom and buzzed her friends in. "I love my friends, I love my family, I love a sunny day!" Riley walked over to the breakfast table, hugged her father around the shoulders, pressed her cheek against his, and declared, "I even love going to school." Riley smiled, thinking about her crush, Lucas, who was the real reason she was a walking, talking rainbow.

Mrs. Matthews glanced sideways at Riley as she sat down to join her family for breakfast.

"Okay, what's going on with her?" Mr. Matthews asked his wife.

"I don't know," Mrs. Matthews replied, wide-eyed. "Don't do anything."

"I'm in a good mood," Riley explained, snapping her fingers and grooving to the beat of the happy tune playing in her head. "This life thing? I think I got it down."

As Maya and Farkle walked through the front door, Mrs. Matthews stood up and grabbed another bowl. "Maya. Oatmeal," she said, holding the bowl out to Riley's best friend.

"No thanks, Mrs. Matthews," Maya replied, still standing by the door.

"Oh, I wasn't asking," Mrs. Matthews said matter-of-factly.

"Yow." Maya walked over and took a seat to Riley's right on the dining table bench. Farkle closed the front door and trailed behind her.

"Farkle, you too," Mrs. Matthews said.

"Thank you," Farkle said with a shrug, "but my mother already made me eggs, home fries, wheat toast, marmalade, and a strawberry shaped like a star."

Everyone else glared at Mrs. Matthews, letting the oatmeal dribble off their spoons and into their bowls, as Farkle sat down to Riley's left on the dining table bench.

"I'm going to the Farkles'!" Auggie shouted, ready to lead an angry breakfast revolt as he got up from his chair. "Who's with me?"

"Sit down," Mrs. Matthews commanded her son and pointed at his bowl. "Eat it, please."

"But it's still *this*." Auggie frowned at the oatmeal.

"Hey, Auggie, guess what?" Mr. Matthews changed the subject. "It's Googly time!"

"No TV at the table," Mrs. Matthews begged her husband.

"You're right, Topanga." Mr. Matthews agreed almost too emphatically. "This table is about the discussion of today's events *only*. Riley—?"

"I woke up, I love everything, I sat here," Riley said with a huge, satisfied grin.

"All caught up." Mr. Matthews shrugged and raised his eyebrows at his wife, securing her silent okay before picking up the remote. "Googly time!"

Everyone turned to watch the small TV sitting on the counter, bopping their heads as they sang along to the theme song: "Here comes Mr. Googly, and his foogly, boogly friends!"

But Auggie didn't join them. Instead, he walked over to the TV and turned it off.

"Hey!" the entire table protested.

"I'm too old for Mr. Googly," Auggie insisted, spinning around on his little black slippers and marching over to the couch.

"What?" Mrs. Matthews demanded, getting up and following her little boy.

"But, Auggie, Mr. Googly's your best friend!" Mr. Matthews pointed out.

"Auggie," Mrs. Matthews said, picking up a giant, fuzzy blue toy. She sat down next to her son and made the toy dance around so that its pink-and-green striped legs and big googly eyes shook, and then she spoke for the toy in a high-pitched voice: "I'm your foogly, boogly best friend!"

"Can I tell you a secret?" Auggie whispered to Mr. Googly.

"Of course." Mrs. Matthews nodded. "You can tell Mr. Googly *all* your secrets."

"I have a new best friend now," Auggie continued in a hushed voice.

"Oh, really? Who would *that* be?" Mrs. Matthews couldn't hide her curiosity.

"I don't want to tell you who she is."

"*She?*" everyone at the breakfast table practically shouted in unison.

"I said too much," Auggie whispered to Mr. Googly.

"Okay," Mrs. Matthews said carefully. "Why

don't you tell Mr. Googly all about your new best friend and none of us will listen?"

Mrs. Matthews played it cool, and the others all pretended to focus on their breakfast, hoping Auggie would take that as a sign that they were giving him some privacy.

"I'm *this* many," Auggie told the toy, holding up five fingers. "I'm done with you now. Good-bye." He took Mr. Googly from his mother and tossed him facedown on the couch.

"They grow up so fast," Riley said, shaking her head glumly at the others.

Not that she was going to let her little brother's newfound maturity introduce any dark clouds into her day. Her world was as perfect as perfect could be, and nothing could possibly ruin it.

CHAPTER 2

Riley felt positively giddy as she and Maya walked through the halls of John Quincy Adams Middle School and over to their lockers. Even the first period warning bell sounded like beautiful music to her ears that morning.

"I was so worried about this new school year," Riley said to her best friend, shaking her long, dark hair. "New school, new people. I didn't think I was going to survive. But not only am I surviving—I'm thriving! I'm like a plant, going like *this*. . . ." Riley shifted her books over to her left arm and did her best plant impression, winding and stretching her right arm overhead while bending her left leg and shaking it behind her. "What was I so worried about?"

Maya simply laughed at her friend as she arrived at the door to history class. But when she peeked in, she stopped short, and Riley nearly bumped into her. Then Maya turned around and put her hands over Riley's eyes, pushing her away from the classroom and against the wall next to the lockers.

"What are you doing?" Riley demanded. "Oh, wait, this is too easy! It's Maya! I know because I saw you put your hand over my face. I'll do you now!"

Riley reached her hands out to try to cover Maya's eyes.

"No, that's not the game," Maya told her.

"What's the game?" Riley asked.

"The game is . . . Protect the Plant from the Bulldozer in the Pink Sweater," Maya said.

Huh? What kind of a game is that?

"Oh, Maya." Riley shook her head at her best friend's silliness, pushing past her and into the classroom. "Bulldozers don't wear pink—" As soon as Riley looked into the classroom, the game finally made sense. And it wasn't a fun game at all. There, sitting on top of their desks, giggling as they stared into each other's eyes, were Lucas and Missy Bradford. He looked adorable as ever in a brown long-sleeved shirt, while Missy looked far *less* adorable in a lace-trimmed leopard-print mini-dress and—yes—a *pink sweater.*

"Huh." Riley chewed on her lower lip and felt tears beginning to burn her eyes as she spun around and walked back into the hall.

"You okay?" Maya asked as Riley slumped against a yellow locker.

"Yeah," Riley lied. The dark clouds were rolling in quickly and there was nothing she could do about them. She slid farther and farther down the locker until she was sitting on the cold, hard ground, hoping against hope that it would swallow her whole.

Maya slid down the wall until she was seated next to Riley. "Awww, look what the bulldozer did to ya," she said with a sympathetic frown.

Riley knew she had to shake it off—that she needed to put the whole thing in perspective. "There are other girls in this world," she said, as much to herself as to Maya, hugging her books close to her chest.

"There are," Maya agreed.

"And other girls—like *Missy Bradford*—are going to talk to Lucas."

"They are." Maya nodded sadly.

"I don't like that."

"I know."

"I wish the world was just me and you." Riley frowned and turned to look hopefully into her best friend's kind blue eyes.

"Then it is," Maya insisted.

Riley rested her head on Maya's shoulder. As much as she wanted her wish to come true, and as much as she wanted to believe Maya's words, she knew better than that. So much for having the whole life thing figured out.

CHAPTER 3

Riley's head felt thick and fuzzy as she sat in the front row of history class. Her dad was standing at the chalkboard, where the words PEARL HARBOR were written in large block letters.

"Sneak attack," Mr. Matthews said to the students, but Riley couldn't hear him. "December 7th, 1941."

"A date which will live in infamy!" Farkle chimed in, raising his index finger.

"A date?" Riley lamented as the word registered in her brain. She turned to look at Maya and caught a brief, painful glimpse of Missy tossing her long brown hair and smiling coyly at Lucas. "They're going on a date? In Italy?"

"No, honey." Maya put a reassuring hand on Riley's arm. "You're in history."

"I'm *history*?" Riley felt the tears starting to burn her eyes again. How had this happened? *Why* had this happened? Her relationship with Lucas had ended before it had even really begun.

"Okay, put your hand up." Maya grabbed Riley's limp arm and lifted it for her.

"Yes, Riley?" Mr. Matthews called on his daughter. "You have a pertinent observation on the subject of the sneak attack?"

Riley stared blankly at Maya, unsure what she was supposed to say, her arm still raised but beginning to droop over her head.

Maya prompted Riley, feeding her the words "May I be excused?" as she pushed her best friend's arm back down to her desk.

"My eyes see my shoes?" Riley jumbled up Maya's words, groggily looking down at the ground.

Mr. Matthews shot a questioning look at Maya, who shook a thumb in the direction of Lucas and Missy. As the teacher observed the way his students were flirting with each other, his dark eyes filled with understanding and he turned back to look at his daughter. "Yes, Riley, you may be excused."

"Forever?" Riley's bleary eyes pleaded with her dad.

"No, you have to come back to class at some point, honey. You just have to."

Somehow Riley managed to pull herself up from her desk and began to stagger toward her father at the front of the classroom. When she nearly walked straight into him, he pushed her just hard enough to steer her toward the door. Then he turned back to the class to continue with the day's lesson.

"It was another sunny day in paradise before the sneak attack that changed everything," Mr. Matthews said.

As he spoke, Riley made her way out into the hall and peered at Lucas and Missy through the long classroom window. She widened her eyes in shock as she watched them continue to flirt . . . and flirt . . . and flirt.

"Do you like the movies?" Missy asked Lucas with a giggle. "It's dark in the movies."

"Depends on the movie," Lucas replied with a shrug. "Depends who I'm going with."

"Scary movies? I get scared at scary movies," Missy cooed, playing with the pencil in her hand. "You'll take care of me, though, right?"

Lucas gave a halfhearted nod, but with her face pressed up against the glass, all Riley could see was that he was falling hard for Missy. Too hard.

Meanwhile, Mr. Matthews kept on talking. "People who had viewed themselves as safe no longer had any security at all," he said.

Still processing Missy's last question, Lucas turned to her and asked, "Just you and me, Missy?"

"Just you and me, Lucas," Missy confirmed. She dropped her pencil onto her desk, leaned over, and tapped her finger on the end of his nose with a playful "Boop!"

Seeing Missy do that jolted Riley out of the shaken, miserable daze she'd been in. She'd seen enough. Missy had gone too far! Riley, now a boiling cauldron of rage, stormed back into the classroom and headed straight for the bulldozer in the pink sweater.

"*Boop?*" Riley demanded, glaring at Missy. "That's the best you got?"

"Please be cool, please be cool, please be cool," Maya muttered, desperately trying to channel a message to her best friend.

"You don't think that I can do *boop*?" Riley laughed in Missy's face.

Maya turned around to look at Farkle. "How bad do you think this is going to be?"

"I think we should have some faith in our Riley," Farkle replied sweetly.

"I can do boop like you've never seen," Riley insisted as she turned toward Lucas.

"Boop!" Riley declared—but as she attempted to give his adorable nose a light tap, the result was a big, giant *oops*. She completely missed the tip of his nose and wound up with her finger directly *inside* it!

No. No. No!

Riley didn't know what to do. She stood frozen in place, unable to move—let alone remove her finger from Lucas's nose.

"You think anybody sees this?" Riley asked Maya in a panic.

"*Everybody* sees this," Missy purred with a self-satisfied smirk.

"Take your finger out!" Maya hissed at Riley, while Lucas just sat there grinning awkwardly.

"Can't. Can't move. Scared," Riley stammered. "Do you think Lucas knows?"

The entire class was now staring at Riley, and Mr. Matthews couldn't possibly continue the lesson with his jaw raking the ground.

"Riley, I've never seen anything like this before," Maya said with a slow, deeply concerned shake of her head. "I don't know what's going to happen."

"Farkle?!" Riley turned to her other friend, desperate for some assistance.

"Boy, Riley, I don't think I could do that even if

I tried," Farkle replied in wide-eyed shock. Then he reached out for Maya's nose and said, "Hey, Maya—boop! Oh, no!"

As it turned out, Farkle *could* do that. So there Riley and Farkle stood, with their fingers in the noses of Lucas and Maya.

If that weren't awkward enough, though, Mr. Matthews had managed to pull himself together and decided to keep talking. "The bombing of Pearl Harbor was our official entrance into a world at war, and nothing would ever be the same," he said.

The word *bombing* bounced around in Riley's head as her dad continued to teach the class. All she could think about now was the fact that that was exactly what she was doing with Lucas—*bombing*. But no matter how desperately she wanted to retreat, she was already in too deep. Just like her finger, which she still had yet to remove from Lucas's nose.

CHAPTER 4

Later that day, Maya and Farkle stood outside Riley's locker. Riley, on the other hand, was *inside* her locker—all the way inside, with her knees scrunched up against her chest and her arms folded against either side of her head, hands over her ears. She looked like a sad doll someone had stuffed into a cabinet.

"You want me to bring you lunch?" Farkle asked her.

"No," Riley groaned. "Food would only keep me alive."

"C'mon, little plant," Maya said with a pout

while leaning against a locker. "Come back into the sun."

"I'm afraid something terrible will happen if I ever come out of here," Riley insisted.

"Riley, that's crazy!" Maya shook her head and laughed in spite of herself. "Nothing could be worse than what's already happened."

But then things *did* get worse, because up walked Missy Bradford.

"Oh, there you are," Missy said, glancing down at Riley. "I've been looking for you. You're not upset with me, are you? Because I didn't hear that you and Lucas were together or anything."

"We're not," Riley replied flatly.

"Yeah, that's what I thought," Missy noted in her overly breathy, I'm-hotter-than-everyone voice. "So if you're not, then it's not a problem if I ask Lucas out. Because he's really cute, don't you think?"

Riley was too upset to respond, but thankfully Maya was right there to speak on her behalf. "I loathe you," Maya told Missy with a tight, spiteful smirk.

"Well, Lucas doesn't," Missy calmly pointed out with a smug smile. "In fact, I think he's kind of into me. *Shocker.*" With that, Missy turned on her heel and walked away like the Wicked Witch of the West.

"I live here now," Riley told her friends.

If only they could have gotten the locker door closed, she would have gladly stayed in there for the rest of her life.

CHAPTER 5

Back at the apartment that evening, Mr. Matthews sat at the dining table working on his laptop. Meanwhile, Mrs. Matthews raced through the sunken living room, chasing after Auggie in his white T-shirt, boxers, and slippers.

"C'mon! PJ time!" Mrs. Matthews called, waving around a pair of bright blue pajamas.

"No, thank you!" Auggie shouted as he rounded the front of the big brown couch.

"Oh, come on, what's tonight's thing?" Mrs. Matthews asked, gaining on her little boy.

"No more PJs!" Auggie insisted, making his way around the back of the couch.

"But they have Mr. Googly on them!"

"I can't wear those anymore," Auggie told his mother as he dove onto the plush couch, right into his Mr. Googly toy.

"Why not?" Mrs. Matthews asked, plopping down next to Auggie.

"Because she won't like them," Auggie told his mother.

"Hey," said Mrs. Matthews, shocked at her son's explanation. "I'm the only 'she' in your life who gets to see you in your pajamas."

"Ya never know," Auggie replied.

Mr. Matthews got up from the dining table and headed over to the couch to help his wife with that one. "Auggie, do us a favor and don't grow up so fast, okay?"

"I need to," Auggie declared, turning toward Mrs. Matthews. "I need to be grown-up and go to bed like Daddy does."

"Uh, how does Daddy go to bed?" Mrs. Matthews laughed nervously.

"Like this." Auggie stood up, spread out his arms, and dove backward onto the couch as he shouted, "Ohhh, *mama*!"

Mr. Matthews's face clouded over with confusion as he pointed at his son. "I don't do *that*," he insisted.

"Yeah, ya do," Auggie replied.

"Every night," Mrs. Matthews agreed with a nod.

"Yeah, but I do it better than that," Mr. Matthews said hopefully.

"If you say so." Mrs. Matthews smirked.

"Auggie, can I at least have my good-night kiss? Okay?" Mr. Matthews tried to change the subject and leaned in for a smooch from his son, but he was denied.

"We're not going to do that anymore," Auggie told his father, backing his face away.

Mr. Matthews looked heartbroken as his wife stood up and tried to soften the blow with the best explanation she could offer: "It's . . . tonight's thing."

"Kissing's for babies. Men shake hands." Auggie

turned from one parent to the other, extended his arm, and shook each of their hands as he said, "Good night, Father. Good night, Mother."

Auggie plopped down onto the couch, but Mr. Matthews was as confused as ever. "What's happening?" he asked his wife.

"Don't take it personally, Cory," she said in a hushed voice. "He thinks he's being an adult."

"How can he be an adult? *I'm* not an adult!" Mr. Matthews tried to contain his frustration, but his voice got louder with each word until he was practically yelling. But then he softened his tone, picked up the fuzzy blue toy, and handed it to his son. "Auggie, please, take Mr. Googly, okay?" Mr. Matthews begged his little boy.

Auggie took the toy, and for a moment it seemed like he was finally about to snap out of whatever phase he was going through. But then he looked deep into Mr. Googly's eyes and said, "Good-bye." He dropped the toy on the ground and marched off to his room.

Mr. and Mrs. Matthews exchanged looks of complete devastation. Their little boy was only five years old! He couldn't be growing up already. They couldn't be losing him yet. They just *couldn't*.

CHAPTER 6

The night air felt cool as it drifted in through the bay window of Riley's room. Maya and Riley sat on the purple cushions of the window seat, trying to come up with a way to fix the mess that had been started earlier that day by a bulldozer in a pink sweater.

"I think of this as a personal challenge issued by Missy Bradford, to grow up and grow up fast," Riley told her best friend. "So what do I do?"

"Nothing," Maya said with a dismissive shrug.

"Give me advice! You're a genius at this. Grow me up!"

"Why?" Maya got a sour look on her face.

"Because everybody else is!"

"That's not the way I see it."

"How can you see it any other way?" Riley demanded.

"Missy Bradford has decided to grow up fast. That has nothing to do with you," Maya explained.

"But what if Lucas takes her to a scary movie?" Riley asked, and then launched into her best breathy-voiced Missy Bradford impression: "'I get scared at scary movies. You'll take care of me, won't you?'" Just thinking about the whole thing made Riley's stomach turn. "Barf! Barf, I say!"

Maya laughed kindly at her best friend. "Riley, do you want Lucas to take you to the movies?"

"Alone?" As much as Riley liked Lucas, going out on an actual *date* with him kind of made her stomach turn, too—in a freaked-out-more-than-grossed-out way. "I don't know if I'm ready for that."

"Then what *do* you want from him?" Maya asked.

"I don't know. I just—I don't want him with her," Riley stammered. All of these feelings were so new and crazy, she didn't even recognize some of them. "Am I jealous?"

"You wouldn't know how to be jealous." Maya shook her head.

"I just—I don't want him taken from us," Riley said desperately. "She's bad news. Teach me how to flirt."

Riley tilted her head, ran a hand through her thick, dark hair, and tried to wink at Maya. Her best friend laughed as she returned the wink and said, "Not gonna do that."

"Why not?"

"*I* don't even know how to flirt. Who our age knows how to flirt?"

Right on cue, Farkle appeared at the open window and offered up his smoothest possible "Hello, ladies," before climbing in and taking a seat next to Maya.

"Farkle!" Riley cringed at the thought of someone else hearing what she and her best friend had just been discussing. "You were out there?"

"I'm always out there," Farkle said with a shrug.

This was actually perfect. More than perfect. How had it not already occurred to Riley? "Farkle, you're the biggest flirt in seventh grade," she said.

"Thank you." Farkle smiled his most flirtatious smile.

"Can you teach me how to flirt with Lucas?"

"I would do whatever you asked me."

"But I thought you loved her," Maya said with a confused look.

"I love both of you," Farkle noted. "I want you both happy."

Awww. Riley shot a grateful look at Farkle and Maya as relief washed over her. She had the best friends in the whole world! Things were looking up—or at least they would be after Farkle taught her how to flirt. Then she could get Lucas away from Missy Bradford and everything would go back to normal. Maybe even better than normal. Not that Riley even knew what normal was anymore.

CHAPTER 7

Sitting at her usual cafeteria table with Maya, Riley picked at the mashed potatoes on her plate. Her eyes darted around the room from one group of kids to another.

"So do you think he'll sit with us . . . or *her*?" Riley lost her appetite as soon as the thought of Missy Bradford entered her head.

"I try not to think about things I have no control over," Maya replied.

"Really? Because that's all I do."

"Hey, can I sit with you guys?" Farkle asked as he approached the table.

"You *better*," Riley told him.

"So," Farkle said, taking a seat and getting down to business. "You think he'll sit with us . . . or *her*?"

Riley fought back a giggle, beyond grateful for Farkle's support.

"Hey, is there a seat with you guys?" Lucas asked as he walked up.

Riley's heart skipped a beat when she turned around in her seat to gaze up at him. *Swoon.* His aqua-green shirt matched the color of his eyes perfectly. "Always room for you, *buddy!*" The moment she said the words, she wished she could take them back. She turned to Maya and frantically whispered, "I said 'buddy.' I'm not helping myself, am I?"

Just as Lucas pulled up a chair next to Riley, Missy Bradford breezed up behind them. She wore an even tighter pink sweater than yesterday's, along with a black-and-white houndstooth miniskirt.

"Well, y'know," Missy said, linking an arm through Lucas's, dragging him out of his chair, and guiding him over to another table, "I was just thinking that if you and I are going to the movies together, I should find out what kind of snacks you like so I could buy some for you because . . ." She pushed Lucas down into a chair and placed a hand on his shoulder for balance. Then she leaned over to adjust one of her black kneesocks, drawing way too much attention to her leg. "I wouldn't want you paying for everything."

"You're toast," Farkle said to Riley.

"I know," Riley replied hopelessly.

"Are you saying she flirts better than you?" Maya asked Farkle.

"Oh, nobody's better than Farkle. I just don't think my young protégé is ready for that monster," Farkle explained in a huff.

"So what're ya gonna do, genius?" Maya smiled at Farkle.

"I think I'll just steal her from Lucas myself," he replied with a grin.

"You would do that for me?" Riley knew she had the best friends in the world, but getting that close to Missy Bradford seemed above and beyond the call of duty.

"Well, I'm certainly not doing it for *me*, toots!" Farkle retorted. "She's evil. If I'm not back in two minutes, she ate me." Before heading into battle, he stopped to ask, "How's my hair?"

"Hasn't changed in six years," Maya said with a sweet smile.

"She doesn't stand a chance!" Farkle declared, tossing his head so his reddish-brown locks whipped against his face.

Farkle walked over to where Missy and Lucas were sitting. "Hello, lady," he said forcefully to Missy.

"Farkle," Missy replied, amused.

"Why go to the movies with a boy, when you can go with"—Farkle swung his leg around to place a gray sneaker on the red lunch table in front of Missy, then tugged up his corduroy pants to expose his thin white calf before concluding—"a man. Enjoy!"

"Wow, look at you," Missy purred, gazing into Farkle's eyes. "You're next."

Farkle raced back over to the table where Riley

and Maya were sitting, panic flashing in his eyes. "It worked. I'm next."

"Riley, she's too good," Maya told her best friend apologetically. "You can't compete with her."

"I don't want them together. I don't!" Riley had to do something about this. And fast. She got up from the table and marched over to where Lucas and Missy were sitting. "Lucas?"

"Riley?"

"I don't know what's going on here, and I don't have any right to say this, but . . . I don't think you should hang out alone with this girl."

Lucas smiled up at Riley. "Why not?"

"I don't really know, but I think if you actually spend time with her alone, it's gonna change things for, you know"—Riley paused and glanced back at Maya and Farkle—"all of us."

Lucas continued to smile at Riley as Missy interjected, "Well, aren't you just the concerned friend?"

"Yeah. I am."

"Well, with you around how could I ever possibly get Lucas alone?" Missy kept her brown eyes fixed on Riley as she dug her hands into the plate of mashed potatoes in front of Lucas. Then she smashed the potatoes onto Lucas's face and her own and shouted, "Food fight!"

"Hey!" Lucas protested.

"No food fight!" Mr. Matthews rushed over, glaring at Lucas and Missy. "Detention. This afternoon. Both of you."

Lucas sighed with frustration, but Missy kept her wide-eyed, mock-innocent gaze fixed on Riley. "Oh, no. Both of us. *Alone*."

How could this be happening? Missy had bulldozed right over Riley again! Maya was right: the girl was too good. But Riley still refused to believe that she couldn't compete with her. She may have lost the battle, but she was determined to win the war.

CHAPTER 8

Leaning against a desk in her dad's classroom, just the two of them, Riley glared at her father. After all, he was the one who had given Lucas and Missy detention. He was the one responsible for making sure that they would get to be alone together! What was he going to do next, plan their wedding?

"How could you do that, Dad?" Riley demanded.

"What did I do?" Mr. Matthews fired back, totally oblivious.

"You gave them detention together!"

"I was the cafeteria monitor," Mr. Matthews tried to explain. "I saw potatoes not where potatoes were supposed to be. Detention her, detention him!"

"But Lucas didn't even do anything," Riley said, hoping her father would see the error of his ways and only Missy would wind up being punished.

"I don't care. I'm mad with power." Mr. Matthews shrugged and turned away from his daughter.

"Then I want detention, too."

"Ya dooo?" Mr. Matthews turned back around, confusion and amusement flashing across his face. "Riley, you've never had detention in your whole life. What could you possibly do that would get you detention on such short notice?"

Fortunately, Riley had already planned for this possibility. "I could introduce you to my special guest star," she told her dad, extending an arm toward the classroom door.

"Uh-oh," Mr. Matthews muttered as Maya walked in, right on cue, and jumped onto his back.

"Nothin' personal, bub," Maya tried to assure him as she forced the teacher down onto his knees.

Just as planned, Riley walked over and twiddled her dad's lips with her finger, forcing him to make an *uh-buh-uh-buh-uh-buh* noise.

"Yeah, that'll do it," Mr. Matthews said.

Yes! Victory! Riley thought with a self-satisfied smile.

"Nice job," Mr. Matthews said, still kneeling on the ground, as he turned around to shake Maya's hand.

"Pleasure doing business with ya," Maya replied.

With that success under her belt, Riley couldn't wait to put the rest of her battle plan into action.

CHAPTER 9

Back at the apartment, Mrs. Matthews sat on the living room couch, reading a book. When Auggie walked up and plopped down next to her, she couldn't believe her eyes. He was wearing his best khaki pants and dark vest over a button-down shirt and shiny black dress shoes.

"Oh, my gosh! Look at you," she said to her little boy.

"How's my breath?" Auggie asked, exhaling like a dragon directly into his mom's face.

"Oooh, like flowers. How'd you do that?"

"I ate your flowers." Auggie paused while Mrs. Matthews considered this. "Mommy?"

"Yeah?"

"You're an older woman, right?"

"Okay," Mrs. Matthews said slowly. "Where's this going?"

"I have an older woman coming over," Auggie explained. "Her name is Ava, she likes cheese, and I'm in *love* with her!"

"Really?" Mrs. Matthews tried not to look too shocked. "Where is Ava from?"

"She's from down the hall. You think you could find some cheese and make yourself scarce?"

As Mrs. Matthews began laughing, the doorbell rang and a look of panic flashed across Auggie's face.

"Too late! She's here!" he shouted and began shaking so hard he made *aguggah-guggah* gurgling noises.

"Okay, okay, okay, calm down," Mrs. Matthews told Auggie as he got up and raced to the door with her following after him. "Women like it when you're calm. Take a deep breath, and then open the door. I can't wait to meet your older woman!"

When Auggie opened the door, there was an adorable little girl with blond curls wearing a purple-and-pink polka-dotted dress. "Hi, Auggie!" the little girl said with a squeaky voice and a little wave.

"Hi, Ava!" Auggie waved back and then pointed backward. "This is my mommy."

"It's so nice to meet you, Ava," Mrs. Matthews said, but Ava stared right through her.

"You got cheese?" Ava demanded, pushing past them and into the apartment. "I like cheese."

"So I've heard," Mrs. Matthews replied, trying not to be too taken aback as she closed the door and followed Auggie and Ava over to the kitchen. "So, Ava, how old are you?"

"I'm *this* many," Ava replied, holding up five fingers and a thumb.

"I see." Mrs. Matthews nodded and forced a tight smile. "Older woman."

"Yeah, because Auggie's *this* many," Ava noted, holding up just five fingers.

"Yeah, but you like him anyway, right?" Mrs. Matthews widened her eyes hopefully.

"Yeah," Ava replied in a singsong voice.

"How come?" Mrs. Matthews suddenly felt like maybe this Ava kid wasn't all that bad.

"Because *this* many tells *this* many what to do," Ava explained, holding up six fingers followed by five fingers.

The smile froze on Mrs. Matthews's face as her heart sank. "What?"

"I'm okay with it, Mom," Auggie insisted.

"Really?" Mrs. Matthews asked, crossing her arms. "Because I have some thoughts."

"Is that a Mr. Googly?" Ava clearly had no interest in those thoughts as she turned around and saw the fuzzy blue toy sitting at the kitchen counter.

"N-no," Auggie stammered.

"I think it is," Ava said, picking up the toy and hugging it to her chest.

"It's not mine," Auggie lied. "I'm too old for it."

"I want it!" Ava said.

"What? Ava, why would you want a Mr. Googly? You're this many," Auggie said, holding up six fingers.

"I *love* Mr. Googly," Ava cooed, widening her eyes. "I'm taking him."

"But you're all growed up!" Auggie waved his arms around, completely thrown off.

"I don't care." Ava shrugged. "He's mine now."

Mrs. Matthews had been quietly watching this exchange while preparing cheese and crackers in the kitchen, but she couldn't stay out of it any longer. "Actually, Ava, what you're gonna do is give Mr. Googly back to Auggie."

"Why would I do that?" Ava said with a sour look.

"Because I'm *this* many," noted Mrs. Matthews, flashing all ten fingers three times. "And *this* many gets to tell *this* many what to do," she concluded, holding up six fingers.

Auggie reached out and took Mr. Googly back.

"Do you like rides?" Mrs. Matthews asked Ava.

"Yeah," Ava replied.

"Oh, great!" Mrs. Matthews picked up Ava and carried her to the door. "Let's take a ride all the way back to your house!"

"Bye-bye, Auggie!" Ava shouted and waved as Mrs. Matthews plunked her down just outside the door.

"Bye-bye, Ava!" Auggie shouted and waved back.

"Okay, bye-bye, Ava," Mrs. Matthews said to Ava.

"Bye!" Ava shouted one last time as Mrs. Matthews closed the door and heaved a giant sigh of relief.

"So, what'd you think of her?" Auggie asked his mom.

Mrs. Matthews stood there, speechless. If this was the sort of girl who appealed to Auggie at a mere five years old, there were going to be a whole lot of rides—bumpy rides—in their future.

CHAPTER 10

Back in the history classroom after school, Riley and Maya sat and doodled on paper while Mr. Matthews graded papers at his desk.

When Missy walked through the door, followed by Lucas, Riley looked up and smiled broadly. "How ya doin'?"

"What are *you* doing here?" Missy demanded, the expression on her face the exact opposite of Lucas's amused one.

"Oh, I'm a bad girl," Riley replied in her most dangerous-sounding voice.

"Yeah, you don't want to mess with this one," Maya agreed.

"What are these?" Missy sneered, picking up the yellow name card Riley had created for Maya with colorful paper and puffy alphabet stickers. "Place cards?"

"Yup, I made them." Riley nodded, pleased with her clever plan to put herself, Lucas, and Maya together. She pointed to a desk in the back of the room, where she'd stuck Missy's card—a pink one, with ugly black letters scrawled on it. "You sit over there."

"I think *this* seat has my name on it, actually," Missy retorted, plunking herself down at the desk next to where Lucas had seated himself.

Before anyone could protest, Mr. Matthews got up and addressed the group. "All right, guys, I like my detention to have a little learnin' in it. So I'd like to continue talking about Pearl Harbor, and what happened after the sneak attack."

Riley began taking notes as her father continued to speak. "The world was at war, and alliances were forged in battle and remained stronger because of that."

Riley and Maya exchanged glances as Farkle appeared in the open doorway. "What is this place?" Farkle asked, walking in.

"It's detention, Farkle. It's not for you," Mr. Matthews said.

"If my friends are in it, then it's for me!" Farkle rushed inside and took a seat behind Riley.

Mr. Matthews wasn't exactly opposed to having another student there to sponge up the knowledge he was imparting, so he continued with the lecture, unfazed. "During this war, the United States was put to one of its greatest tests when it met a threat to our way of life. But because we were united, we prevailed."

As Riley considered her father's words—*united, prevailed*—Lucas called over to her. "Hey, Riley, Missy invited me to see a movie with her."

Riley's heart sank. Why was he reminding her?

"I think she's aware of that, Lucas," Missy interjected. "No need to make her feel worse."

"And I was wondering if maybe you guys would

like to come along with us," Lucas added, motioning to Riley, Maya, and Farkle. *Oh. Ha!* He wasn't trying to make Riley feel worse, as Missy had suggested. He was too nice for that. Riley never should have doubted him.

"You want us?" Riley asked, just to make sure.

As Lucas nodded, Missy pouted and told him, "I'm sorry, Lucas, that wasn't the invitation."

"Oh. Well, then," Lucas replied, his green eyes sparkling playfully as he continued to look at Riley. "I'm sorry, Missy, but I can't go."

"What are you talking about?" Missy whined. "Nobody's ever turned me down in my life!"

"Well, see, these are my friends," Lucas explained to her carefully. "And I don't like doing anything without my friends. Right, Riley?"

"Yeah." Riley nodded. "Right." She'd already known Lucas was an amazing guy, but this went above and beyond confirming it. Could he be any more perfect?

"Now, I certainly appreciate you wanting me

to take care of you during a scary movie, and you showing me your leg and all," Lucas said sweetly, turning back to look at Missy. "But back here in the seventh grade, I think maybe we'd have more fun just hanging out together."

Missy looked horrified. Disgusted. But best of all, *defeated*.

"Boop!" Maya said with a smirk, pointing a finger at Missy, who looked more like a delicate pink flower than a bulldozer at this point.

"Grow up," Missy fired at all three of them as she stood up and walked out of the classroom in a huff.

"Not. Yet." Riley looked around the room at her friends. Maya had been right the other night: Missy Bradford's growing up fast had *nothing* to do with Riley. It had nothing to do with any of her friends.

"Oh, she's leaving?" Mr. Matthews asked when Missy was gone. "Okay."

"Hey," Riley said to Lucas.

"Hey," Lucas replied.

"You know what the easiest thing about having friends is?" Riley asked him.

"What?" Lucas said.

"Sometimes all you have to do is trust them."

A sense of calm washed over Riley when she realized that she didn't need to worry about losing Lucas—just like she didn't need to worry about losing Maya or Farkle. They cared about each other too much, and Missy Bradford couldn't change that.

Riley hadn't lost the battle *or* the war, and she'd never felt better about what the future held. It was just like what her dad was saying now about Pearl Harbor: "When peacetime came, the United States then enjoyed its greatest period of growth, prosperity, and happiness."

Yeah. It felt good to be happy again.

"Detention over," Mr. Matthews added. "You guys comin'?"

"No. We're good right here," Riley replied.

Sitting there with her friends, she wished she could bottle up that moment and make it last forever—that she could make time stand still, at least for a little while. Of course she knew that was impossible. But at least she could hang on and appreciate the moments they did have, like this one, for as long as they lasted.

CHAPTER 11

As Mr. and Mrs. Matthews sat curled up in the bay window of the living room, looking out at the peaceful night sky, Auggie walked up in his red plaid boxers and white T-shirt.

"Good night, Mother. Good night, Father," Auggie said, extending his hand to shake each of theirs before turning around to head back to his room.

"I'm not sure how much longer I can put up with this," Mr. Matthews said to his wife with a frown.

But almost as soon as Auggie disappeared, he was back again—with Riley, who was carrying him, along with his blue PJs, in her arms.

"Now you listen to me, kid—you take these jammies and you wear them," Riley told her brother, plopping him down on the couch and picking up his fuzzy blue stuffed toy. "And you take Mr. Googly and you hold on to him for as long as you can."

"Why?" Auggie asked with wide-eyed wonder.

"Because he's your friend, you can trust him, and he loves you, right?"

"Yeah. He does," Auggie admitted.

"And, Auggie, it's very important that you hold on to your friends," Mr. Matthews added, coming over to the couch and sitting next to his little boy.

"And, Auggie, stay this way for as long as possible," Mrs. Matthews said, holding up five fingers as she joined the family on the couch. "Because when it's gone, it's gone."

"Good night, buddy," Mr. Matthews said, reaching out his arm to shake Auggie's hand.

But instead, Auggie gave his dad a kiss on the cheek. Then he turned and gave his mother a kiss on hers. "You want one?" he asked Riley.

"Yeah," his sister replied.

"Then you have to catch me!" Auggie shouted, jumping up from the couch and running toward his bedroom.

As Riley chased after her little brother, Mrs. Matthews turned to her husband. "You want one?" she asked with a coy smile.

"Yeah!" Mr. Matthews said eagerly.

"Then you have to catch me!" Mrs. Matthews laughed, leaping up from the couch and running toward their bedroom.

"Oh, *mama!*" Mr. Matthews jumped up and chased after his wife.

When they were all out of the living room, Mr. Googly sat looking lost and all alone on the couch. But not for long. A few moments later, Auggie raced in. He grabbed his fuzzy blue toy, cradled it in his arms, and headed back to his room.

Everything—and everyone—was finally back to how it should be. Nobody wanted to grow up too fast or be anyone other than themselves. It turns out your world gets better when you follow your heart.